Captain McGrew Wants YOU for his Crew!

For Rob – a worthy shipmate! – M.S.

For Dad, land ahoy! – E.E.

Bloomsbury Publishing, London, Oxford, New York, New Delhi and Sydney

First published in Great Britain in 2017 by Bloomsbury Publishing Plc
50 Bedford Square, London WC1B 3DP

www.bloomsbury.com

BLOOMSBURY is a registered trademark of Bloomsbury Publishing Plc

Text copyright © Mark Sperring 2017
Illustrations copyright © Ed Eaves 2017

The moral rights of the author and illustrator have been asserted

A CIP catalogue record of this book is available from the British Library

ISBN 978 1 4088 7105 8 (HB)
ISBN 978 1 4088 7103 4 (PB)
ISBN 978 1 4088 7104 1 (eBook)

All papers used by Bloomsbury Publishing are natural, recyclable products made
from wood grown in well managed forests. The manufacturing processes conform
to the environmental regulations of the country of origin

Printed in China by Leo Paper Products, Heshan, Guangdong

1 3 5 7 9 10 8 6 4 2

Captain McGrew Wants

YOU
for his Crew!

Mark Sperring   **Ed Eaves**

BLOOMSBURY
LONDON OXFORD NEW YORK NEW DELHI SYDNEY

Meet Captain McGrew:
He's in need of a crew
to do all those jobs
that pirate crews do.

You'll need bulging muscles
(strong fingers, strong thumbs)
to HOIST up the main sail
and wave . . .

GOODBYE, MUM!

You **HAVE** to be tough,
that has to be said,
to **PULL** up the anchor
from the sea bed . . .

You mustn't be little
and you mustn't be BIG,

but just the right size to

GET UP
THAT RIG!

You MUST be prepared to SHOUT:

LAND AHOY!

And go by the title of

LAD,

LASS

or BOY!

Can you dig for **LONG** hours while others . . .

CANNOT?

And while Captain McGrew
sits in the cool shade,
can you make him a snack
and SQUEEZE lemonade?

Can you H-EE-EE-AVE out the treasure all by YOURSELF?

Can you SPLOOSH down the POOP DECK?

BATTEN the HATCH?

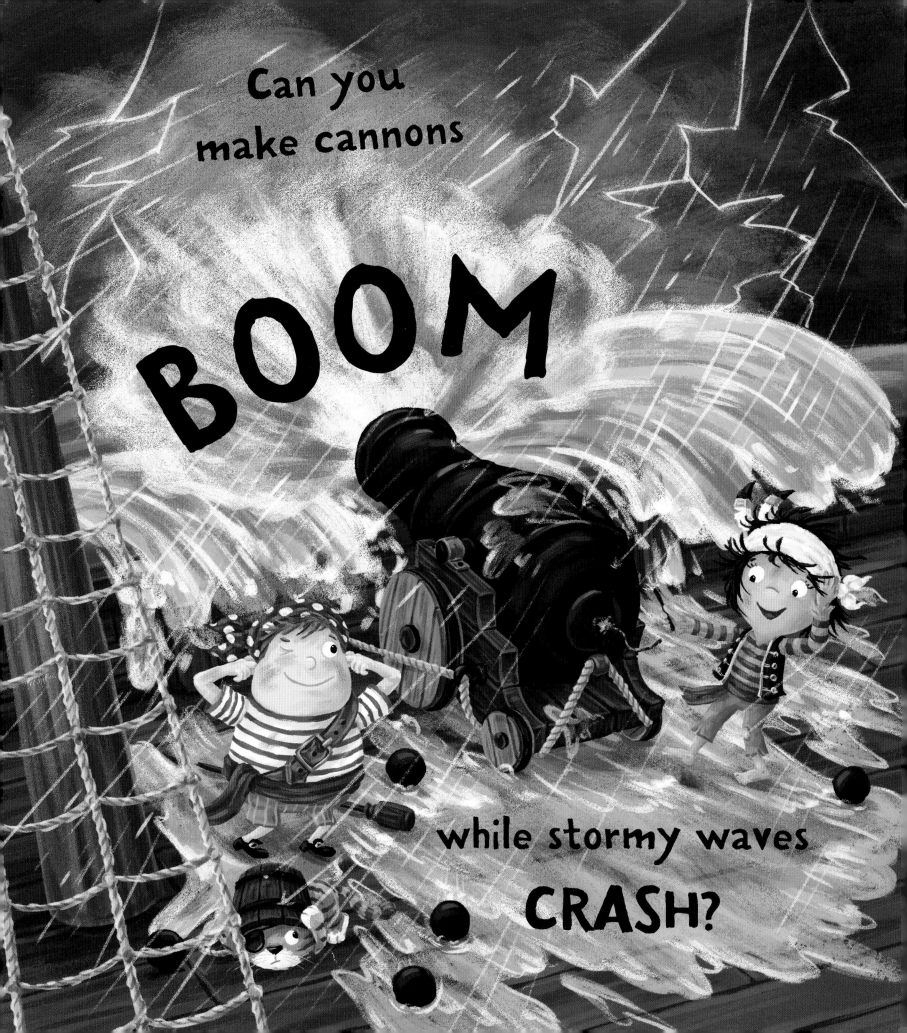

And though you're plum tired, YES, after all THAT, could you go to the galley and heat up a vat?

Then RUSTLE up supper
for Captain McGrew.
Something so simple . . .

like OCTOPUS STEW?

Would you DO THE DISHES with no word of thanks?

Could you clean off the hull,
till it's tidy and neat?

And NEVER,

NO NEVER,

find time for a sleep?

Can you read bedtime stories?

Sing sweet songs you know?

Navigate through the night
as **McGrew** snores below?

I hope you CAN do this,
YES, REALLY, I do,
for I know a pirate who's
picked out his crew . . .

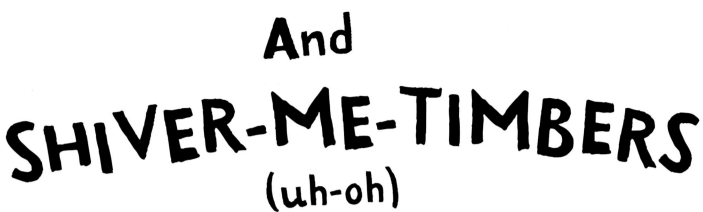

And
SHIVER-ME-TIMBERS
(uh-oh)
IT'S YOU!
YES, Captain McGrew
wants YOU
for his crew!

But for those who **AREN'T** suited
to a life on the waves . . .

there's a knight here
called Norman
who's been looking
for knaves!